W9-BIA-660

Daphne, Secret Vlogger

Daphne, Secret Vlogger is published by Stone Arch Books
A Capstone Imprint
1710 Roe Crest Drive
North Mankato, Minnesota 56003
www.mycapstone.com



Library of Congress Cataloging-in-Publication Data is available on the Library of Congress website.

Summary: Daphne is a hilarious, fashion-savvy YouTube star. But at school, where Daphne is really Annabelle Louis, seventh-grade super geek, wearing the latest trends is far off her radar. Her therapist, Dr. Varma, suggests she try something new—a wardrobe makeover. Fashionable outfits bring Annabelle newfound attention, which she can't help but enjoy. But when her new popular friends start showing their true colors and making fun of others, Annabelle becomes fed up with fashion trends and popularity. Luckily she has her vlog, *Daphne Doesn't,* where she can make fun of it all and be her true self. Meanwhile Annabelle tries to keep her secret identity as Daphne from leaking out, and popular girl Rachael Myers is determined to find out the truth.

ISBN 978-1-4965-6296-8 (library-bound hardcover)
ISBN 978-1-4965-6300-2 (paperback)
ISBN 978-1-4965-6304-0 (eBook PDF)

Cover illustration by Marcos Calo
Design by Kay Fraser

Printed and bound in Canada
PA020

# DAPHNE Definitely DOESN'T DO FASHION

by Tami Charles

STONE ARCH BOOKS
a capstone imprint

efinitely doesn't do sports D
esn't do drama Definitely do
finitely doesn't do fashion D
dances Definitely doesn't do
Definitely doesn't do sports S
esn't do drama Definitely doe
finitely doesn't do fashion D
do dances Definitely doesn't
ly doesn't do sports Definitel
esn't do drama Definitely do
finitely doesn't do fashion D
ances Definitely doesn't do F
ely doesn't do sports Definite
esn't do drama Definitely do
Definitely doesn't do Sports
ances Definitely doesn't do

# 1

# MAKEOVER TIME!

Some fashion disasters require complete obedience. When your mom is a Master Sergeant in the Air Force, but looks hot enough to be Beyoncé's sister, you shut your mouth and take the help.

Exhibit A—me, Annabelle "Daphne" Louis. Dork by day, accidental YouTube star by night. And maybe accident isn't the right term in my case. When my parents moved us from Germany to Linden, New Jersey (and basically ruined my life!), they thought it would be a good idea for me to see a therapist. And why, might you ask? Because for the first time in a long time, I'd be attending real school, not like the homeschool I was used to with Dad. Oh, then there's the fact that Mom's taking off to Afghanistan for six months! So yeah, seeing Dr. Varma is supposed to help me *cope with life's challenges*. And by cope, she means: Make a YouTube channel, try new activities like sports (epic fail #1) and drama (epic fail #2), and ramp up my social skills so I won't look like a sad, sick puppy when Mom abandons me next month.

Turns out that even though sports and dramatic plays weren't my thing, my YouTube viewers enjoyed seeing me make a fool of myself and my views are growing each day. Now Dr. Varma's all on my case and wants me to make a new vlog post about fashion. Because in her mind, maybe *this* will do something amazing for my social life.

How about *not*? I've made three friends

at school—John, Clairna, and Nav—and even though my bestest of all best friends, Mae, is back in the UK, we talk all the time. Thank you, FaceTime!

But it doesn't matter how I feel about this whole makeover experiment—though, not gonna lie, I'm secretly excited—because Mom is all over it as soon I get home.

"Let's pick out something really cute for school tomorrow." She barges into my bedroom, hands full of clothes hangers and the biggest smile on her face.

It's like she's been dreaming of this Cinderella moment all her life.

Mom is a total diva. Flawless ebony skin, straight hair, and outfits worthy of a runway in Milan.

But that's not me. Typically my wardrobe screams, "I prefer staying home!"

"What in the world am I supposed to do with all of this stuff?" I sigh, rummaging through the mounds of clothes.

It looks like *Seventeen* magazine threw up all over my bed.

"Listen, as far as fashion goes, you can keep it simple, Annabelle. I get it. You like to be comfortable."

"Now you're speaking my language. Comfort is something I know all about!" I admit.

And suddenly, I remember our time overseas, on base in the UK. The days of taking math class in our kitchen with Mae and Dad . . . and we all wore pajamas. Homeschool was the best! These days, it's a struggle to find anything to wear that doesn't make me look like I've spent the whole day watching Netflix.

Mom lets me try on some of her old jeans. All cute. And surprisingly they all fit even though Mom is curvy and I look like I'm made of parallel lines.

"Those are great," Mom says.

I check myself out in the full-length mirror hanging on my closet door. She's right. I don't look bad. In fact, I'm pretty sure I saw Rachael—queen of seventh grade—wearing a similar pair of jeans last week.

I leave those on, and Mom starts showing me her shirts. "Since you typically mix your prints, let's try something solid for a change."

She hands me a blush-pink blouse, with just a little frill on the sleeve. Very trendy. Very not me. But I put it on anyway. I look in the mirror again and can't believe how different I already look.

"Mom, this whole outfit looks great!" I say. "It's not even itchy!"

"See? Stylish and comfortable! But there's nothing wrong with dressing casually either. You look beautiful no matter what."

My heart fills and sinks simultaneously. I know she means it, but sometimes I wonder if she says things like that because that's what moms are supposed to say.

"My hair." I sigh and sit in front of my dresser mirror.

"What's wrong with it? I love your hair." Mom runs her fingers through it.

"It's just so poofy. Why can't it be straight, like yours?" I complain.

"Annabelle, my natural hair is curly too. I just use a relaxer because it's easier for my lifestyle. But you know the rules."

"Yeah, yeah, yeah . . . no relaxer before I'm sixteen."

*Three years and counting!*

Mom smiles. "If you want something temporary, I could—"

"Straighten it? Oh, Mom, PLEASE!" I jump out of my seat and hug her. Next thing I know we collapse on the bed.

"OK, Annabelle. I'll straighten your hair, but don't get used to it. Even heated styling tools can damage your hair. And trust me, I know plenty of girls who would pay to have curls like yours."

Mom washes and deep conditions my hair in the laundry room sink. After that she sets up my bedroom with her blow dryer, flat iron, jojoba oil, and some spray in a bottle.

"This is heat protectant spray, so your hair doesn't get damaged from the flat iron." Mom demonstrates how to use the flat iron to straighten my curls. Start at the root and follow with a comb to the ends.

It takes her over an hour to transform my hair from a short mop to long, straight hair that reaches the middle of my back.

"I had no idea my hair was this long!" I scream.

"Natural curls shrink hair to make it look much shorter than it really is," Mom says.

When she is done, she applies a soft pink gloss to my lips.

"Something is missing," Mom says.

"What else could I possibly need? This is perfect! I can't wait to go to school tomorrow."

"Stay here. I'll be right back."

Mom returns with a necklace in her hand. When she puts it on me, I trace it with the tips of my fingers. Navy blue gemstone, heart-shaped, with a silver chain sparkling brighter than the moon in a dark sky. Pure perfection.

"I love this, Mom." My eyes begin to sting. And I'm not sure why, but suddenly I feel warm and happy and sad all wrapped in one.

"My mother gave me this when I was about your age. She was getting deployed and wanted me to have it to think of her while she was gone. I was waiting for the right moment to pass this on to you. I could have done it the other times I left, but those assignments were just a couple weeks here and there. It didn't feel right then. But now that I'll be in Afghanistan for six months, I want you to have it, keep it safe next to your heart, and know that I'm always there."

"I am never, ever taking this necklace off."

*And cue tears!*

Mom's crying. I'm crying.

Dad knocks on my door. "Hey, what are we

boo-hooing about?" he asks, pushing the door open.

Mom shows him the necklace. *My* necklace.

"I was wondering when you'd give it to her. You look stunning, Annabelle," he says.

"Thanks, Dad."

"It's getting late. You should get some sleep. Put your outfit on a hanger and wrap your hair in this silk scarf so it doesn't get frizzy," Mom says.

They say goodnight and close the door behind them.

I rush to my phone to text Mae a selfie of the new me.

**Mae:** Excuse me, who is this? THAT is not Annabelle Louis.

**Me:** I know, ha! It's my new look. You like?

**Mae:** Like? How about LOVE? Especially that necklace! You're like Annabelle version 2.0.

**Me:** Thanks, off to bed. Tomorrow starts my next social experiment: “Daphne Does Fashion.”

**Mae:** You got this, *amiga*!

# 2

# THE NEW KID . . . AGAIN

I step into homeroom, and everyone stops talking. Usually Mrs. Rodriguez has to yell at us to hush our mouths, but not today. As I walk to my seat at the back of the room, I hear the whispers.

"Is that Annabelle?"

"She's not wearing weird clothes today."

"No, I think that's a new student."

Part of me is loving the attention, but there is a small part of me that wants to hop a plane and head straight back to Germany.

Rachael turns around and starts looking me up and down. Just like she did at the school play last month, where she played the lead in *Little Shop of Horrors* and I was her understudy. I arrived ready to fulfill my backstage duties, not realizing that Rachael would get sick and *I'd* have to take over her lead role. She's been acting wishy-washy ever since.

My shoulders tense up, and I give Rachael a shy wave. As soon as I do that, she stops inspecting my entire outfit, smiles back, and turns around in her chair.

"Why are you all dressed up?" John asks.

"Just felt like doing something different," I half-lie.

Confession #1: My therapist and my mom made me do it.

Confession #2: And I kinda like it.

But I don't say that.

John purses his lips like he has more to say, but he doesn't. Instead, he sinks lower in his chair and sticks his nose back in his notebook.

Clairna leans in and whispers, "Look at you, Miss Diva! Don't get too popular on us now." Then she giggles.

I'm wondering if that's the goal here. Am I trying to be popular? Do I even care?

And then that inner voice whispers, *Yes, you do!*

For the rest of my classes, not one of my teachers recognizes me.

"Are you the new kid?"

"Oh, your hair is different!"

Even the school counselor, Mr. Fingerlin, doesn't know who I am at first.

When the lunch bell rings, John, Clairna, and I make our way to the cafeteria. Navdeep is out sick today.

The McManus Café is famous for putting the word "surprise" on the daily lunch menu. Chili dog surprise, pizza surprise, taco surprise. That last one sent me running to the bathroom on the third day of school! My YouTube followers had a good laugh when I made a vlog about that epic fail! These days I keep it safe with good old peanut butter and jelly. We take a seat at our "reserved" table in the back of the cafeteria. Near the garbage, with an added bonus of spoiled-milk aroma.

Clairna and I do most of the talking while John pushes lettuce around his lunch tray and says nothing.

Then Clairna gets all whispery. "Girl, you will never believe who added me on Snapchat over the weekend."

"Oooh, spill it!"

"I'll give you some hints. Soccer team, dark mohawk, sits at queen diva's table . . ." Clairna's voice slows down, and her eyes drift to the side.

I turn around to see what she's looking at.

All of a sudden, Rachael gets up from her table in the middle of the cafeteria and starts strutting her stuff toward us. It's like a scene straight out of a fashion show.

The lights dim, the spotlight is on her. Katy

Perry's "Roar" is playing on the loudest decibel. In slow motion, everyone stops eating and stares at Rachael, who is headed my way.

Everything goes back to regular motion as soon as she gets to our table.

"Annabelle, why don't you come sit with us today?" Rachael says.

A glob of peanut butter settles in my throat.

Clairna looks at me and then softly kicks me under the table. And I'm not sure if that kick means "don't you dare" or "you'd better go, girl!" Then she puckers her lips and shoots her eyes straight to Rachael's table. That's when I know exactly why she wants me to go. . . . *Boys*. John, on the other hand, doesn't even look at me. In fact, he's barely said two words to me all day.

"Umm . . . sure, OK," I say nervously. "Let me grab my things."

I toss out my lunch tray and gulp down half a carton of milk. Because there is no way

I'm sitting at Rachael's table with peanut-butter mouth. Not when all of her friends and some of the boys from the basketball team are sitting there.

Remember that fashion show strut? Well, it starts up all over again, and this time all eyes are on her . . . and me. Rachael walks like she owns the place. I try to swing my hips—as if I had any—but I know I probably look more like a dog being walked on a leash than anything.

"You guys know Annabelle, right?" Rachael says to her groupies when we get to her table.

I wave shyly.

"Oh yeah, your understudy from the play," one of the girls says, laying it on thick with the word *under.*

"Have a seat," Natasha says.

"So, spill it. What's with the new digs?" Rachael wastes no time getting right to business.

Suddenly I feel stupid saying the truth—

that the reason I dressed up is to step out of my comfort zone. Because my therapist and parents think I need to try new things to make new friends.

"Oh, I just have an early dinner tonight with my parents. . . ." I search my brain for more details to spice up the story, "in the city, with my dad's company. He's an executive . . . at Cisco."

Only one-third of that is true. But the rest sounds fabulous enough.

"Ooh nice!" another girl, Lauren, chimes in. "I love going to the city. So chic."

"Where'd you get the necklace?" Natasha moves in a little too close to me, lifting the necklace with her hand.

"From some fancy jewelry store with Daddy's executive credit card?" Rachael asks.

"It's a family heirloom, apparently. My grandmother was in the army. She gave it to my mom when she got deployed. My mom gave it to me because . . ."

I can't even say the rest because I don't want to face the fact that Mom's leaving me. Even if it is only temporary.

"Oh." Rachael shrugs, but doesn't say anything after that. Instead, she sort of shuts down, which is way out of character for her.

Some kids at the table start doing army salutes and making silly fighting poses. And the ring leader of them all? Dark, mohawk cut. Super broad shoulders. Soccer shirt. Stuffing straws up his nose.

Steven Chu. Aka Clairna's new Snapchat buddy.

I feel Clairna eyeing me from across the cafeteria. She winks and mouths, "That's him!"

The bell rings, and Rachael storms out of the cafeteria.

"You can sit with us tomorrow, if you like," Natasha says, gathering her tray and the one Rachael left behind.

I see Rachael running toward the bathroom on the other side of the cafeteria. Meanwhile,

John's eyes are fixed on me and his face is twisted up like he smells something bad.

"Um, yeah, maybe," I say. "Nice chatting with you guys. See you later."

I'm pretty sure John is taking his time throwing away his trash and walking out of the cafeteria because he wants me to catch up to him and say something, but I need to check on Rachael.

When I get to the bathroom, one stall door is closed and I can hear her sniffling.

"You OK in there?"

She flushes the toilet and comes out of the stall. Whatever makeup she had on has been washed away by the tears she tried to hide from me.

"I'm good. You didn't have to follow me in here. I just had something stuck in my eye."

She's a better liar than I am.

"Did I say something wrong when I mentioned the deployment stuff?" I ask. "If so, I'm sorry."

"Oh, it's cool." She shrugs.

"How do you deal?" I ask.

"Deal with what?"

"Everything, I guess. Your dad being deployed."

"You just do. Fill up your time with activities, like hanging out with your friends, going to the movies, shopping. All of that stuff is important too. Besides, why would you care? You have your mom at home with you."

I chew on my bottom lip and then say the words slowly. "My mom's being sent to Afghanistan. TDY."

It's the first time I've told anyone other than Dr. Varma and Mae.

For a second, it looks like Rachael feels sorry for me.

"Well that T for temporary is nothing but a lie." Rachael splashes water on her face. "Anyway, I'm over it." Rachael's voice returns to snob status. Then she whips out her makeup bag and starts *putting her face on* again.

"Why'd you ask me to sit with you at lunch?"

"No reason in particular." Rachael must feel me staring at the way she does her makeup. "Want me to show you a new trend?" she asks.

"Sure," I say.

She pulls out a brown pencil and starts drawing a squiggly line around my eyebrow. Then she fills it in.

"All the style blogs are talking about this." She hands me the pencil so I can draw the other eyebrow. I look in the mirror, carefully drawing it, wondering if I look stylish or plain ridiculous.

Just then a notification sounds off on my phone. I finish up my squiggly brow and hand her back the pencil. When I open the home screen, I see it's a YouTube update. According to their stats, my last video, "Daphne Definitely Doesn't Do Drama," has more than thirty-five thousand views and my channel has nine thousand subscribers. Holy cow! My heart starts racing so fast, I drop my phone on the floor.

Rachael quickly reaches down and grabs it, but not before being nosey.

"Hmm . . . I didn't know you watched that vlog."

"I accidentally followed it. Now I get these silly notifications every now and then."

"You know what I found out about that Daphne girl?" Rachael applies a final coat of lip gloss.

"What's that?" I ask nervously.

"That she lives here."

*Alert! Alert! Somebody call me an ambulance!*

"Um, what do you mean?"

"Like here in Jersey!" Rachael pulls out her phone and scrolls to a comment on YouTube from a screen name I recognize as Mae's. The comment mentions Daphne being a "Jersey Girl." I stop breathing.

"Oh!" I laugh nervously. "But you know, this state is so big."

"How crazy would it be if she lived close to Linden?"

"Totally crazy." But that's all I have to say about that. This Daphne thing is a secret that exists only between me, my parents, Dr. Varma, and Mae. And I plan to keep it that way.

Time to shift the focus.

"Hey, I thought you don't follow her either," I say.

The brown in Rachael's cheeks deepens. "I don't. Remember when the drama teacher showed us one of Daphne's videos at drama rehearsal month?"

The memory rolls in like a movie reel: Clairna and Nicholas getting a notification about my new vlog, them getting caught by Mr. Davis when we should've been working, and then Mr. Davis confiscating the phone to show the WHOLE cast while I tried to hide from the world! Still no one recognized me beneath my Daphne disguise.

"Of course I remember!" I try to play it cool, swallowing the clump of nerves in my throat.

The second bell rings, thank goodness. Just then Clairna and two older kids walk in.

Clairna gives me a wink as she walks to the sink next to where Rachael and I are standing in front of the mirror.

"Hey, I'm going shopping and maybe to the movies with a few friends this weekend," Rachael says. "You should come. I could help you pick out some new clothes, since you're all into fashion now."

*What did she say?* My stomach is doing backflips, but I try to play it cool. I pull a chunk of hair back behind my ear like I see the teens do in rom-com movies.

"Shopping?" My voice is scratchy sounding.

"Bryan will be there." Rachael giggles.

Clairna starts coughing super loud.

Bryan Green. Stats: Sun-kissed skin. Basketball team. Keeps a fresh haircut like he lives in the barbershop. Smells good. Not that I ever stood close enough to tell, but if I did, I bet he'd smell *woodsy*.

"Oh, that's cool. Is Steven Chu going too?" I ask.

*And cue Clairna coughing again!*

Rachael twists her face at Clairna, but doesn't even ask if she's OK.

"No, I don't think so."

Without Rachael noticing, Clairna presses on my foot, gentle at first, then harder.

"*Oww,* I mean, aww . . . that's fine." I curl my toes inside my Mary Janes. "I think I can fit it in my *sched*." I shorten the word because I hear the kids doing that all the time around here.

"Here, take my number." Rachael grabs my phone and types in her info. "Saturday. Four o'clock. Aviation Plaza." And then she heads for the exit.

"Bye. Um, see you around there, I mean then. . . ."

The door slams shut.

"I can't believe you're going shopping with Rachael Myers!" Clairna squeals.

"I tried to work you in there with the Steven angle, but—"

"I heard that. . . . ugh!" Clairna's smile fades. "Whatever. Who cares? Annabelle, I think maybe Rachael's starting to finally see what we've seen all along: that you are one cool chick."

# 3

# DAPHNE GOES SHOPPING

Dad has a conniption mid-drive when I tell him that after shopping, the girls and I are going to the movies "with some guys from school."

"Guys?" His neck goes beet red, and he almost loses control of the steering wheel.

"It's not a big deal, Dad."

Mom butts in. "Put a sock in it, Ruben. Our girl's growing up." She turns to me. "You can go, but we'll pick you up right after the movie is over, you hear?"

"Yes, Mom."

Mom and Dad drop me off at Aviation Plaza, right in front of the Kicks USA store. At first I don't see anyone, so I just stand there waiting.

"If you need us we'll be right there in Target," Dad calls out the window. "I have my phone on me . . . and a baseball bat in the trunk."

Mom starts cracking up.

"Please don't be weird and follow me around," I shout back.

"We promise. Have fun with your new *friends,*" Mom says. Then they finally drive away.

I shuffle around on the sidewalk and stare at the dried leaves scattering across the pavement. A few minutes later, I get a text.

**Rachael:** Hey girl, almost there.

It's not long before a car pulls up and

Rachael, Natasha, and Lauren step out and wave Mrs. Myers off.

"Ready for some shopping, girls?" Rachael yells.

We all laugh and go inside the Kicks store.

"Having a collection of fresh kicks is essential when you're in middle school," Rachael says to me, like I'm a student in her personal fashion academy.

I walk around taking note of every style she suggests, but on the inside, I'm gagging at the prices. One hundred twenty-nine dollars for a pair of sneakers!

"You should try these on." Natasha holds up a pair of Nikes with a sparkly glitter-gold symbol.

Too flashy. Totally not my style, but I just go with it and say, "Sure!"

When I put them on, I still feel the same way, but the girls are *ooh*-ing and *ahh*-ing about how "lit" they are.

"You should get them!" Rachael insists.

I don't tell her that I only have a hundred dollars saved from my allowance.

"I think I'll pass," I say.

"Well if you don't want them, I'm scooping these bad boys up."

Rachael and Natasha grab the same sneakers. I have to get something, so I follow Lauren to the clothing section. She's got her hands full with jeans and tops. I check to make sure no one is watching and head to the clearance rack. I pick up a T-shirt that's on sale for nine dollars.

"That's all you're getting?" Rachael asks when we get to the register.

"Yeah." My cheeks go red. "I'm holding out for the good stuff at the other stores we go to."

"Ah, I see your strategy! You're gonna love Old Navy and Mad Rag."

We pay for our things and then walk out of the store. As we walk, I spot the Second

Chance thrift store. Before I started my Daphne vlog, Mom brought me here to load up on disguises and decorations for my girl cave, where I film everything. It's been a while since I've been to the store and I'm already drooling (and fuming!) at what I see in the display window: a shirt similar to one from Kicks that was almost sixty dollars. But here at Second Chance, it's priced at three dollars. THREE DOLLARS!

Oh, I MUST go in! "Guys, let's check this place out," I say aloud.

Rachael, Lauren, and Natasha make faces like they just smelled fresh roadkill.

"I know you're new to the US and all, so let me school you on some things," Rachael says. "This is a hand-me-down store. The clothes in here are not . . . how would you say . . ."

"Um, *lit*! They're clothes for, like, old people!" Lauren chimes in.

But my hand is already on the door and I'm

halfway into the store. The girls follow me in, probably to change my mind.

I see so many cool things here, and they're begging for me to buy them. With ninety-one dollars left, I could do some real damage in this store. I snatch a burgundy velvet vintage dress off the rack.

"You're kidding, right?" Rachael eyes the dress skeptically.

Just then, I see the lady from the last time I shopped here with Mom—Georgia. Her eyes light up when she recognizes me. And then I remember how Mom told this sweet lady ALL of my business while we were shopping.

I toss the dress back on the rack like it's garbage. "Totally playing with you guys!" I lie as blue as the sky. "Let's go."

"Oh, I thought so," Natasha says.

"Yeah, let's get out of here!" Lauren says.

But Georgia's already moving in on us. "Hey! I remember you!"

The girls give me weird looks. But I keep pushing us along.

That doesn't stop Georgia from following us. "How'd everything go with that show you were working on?" she asks.

Rachael looks at me, confused.

"Oh, the play?" I say. "Yeah, that was fun. Big turnout. Nice seeing you, gotta go!"

I'm really pushing the girls out now, moving farther and farther away from Georgia.

"But I thought it was something with the computer?" she mumbles, and I pray I'm the only one who heard her.

"What was all that about?" Rachael asks as we leave the store.

We cross the parking lot and head to Old Navy. I see Mom and Dad walking into Marshalls, but they don't see me. Thank goodness!

"Um, not really sure. Probably a bad memory!" I say.

"Yeah, old people!" Rachael says.

All the girls start laughing.

I decide I can't afford another slip-up. No sense in being cheap. I'm just going to spend the rest of this money and let Rachael have her way.

The girls help me pick out some things from Old Navy and Mad Rag. Some heeled boots, crushed velvet tops with the shoulders cut out, jeans ripped at the knee, a few bodysuits (suddenly I'm having Sports Day wedgie nightmares all over again), and skirts. The good thing is that most of the stuff they pick out for me is a reasonable price. When we're done, I have thirty-one dollars to spare.

By the time we get to the movies, our hands are full of bags and there are some other kids from McManus waiting around.

We purchase tickets to see *Midnight's Curse*. As Rachael promised, Bryan is there. So are some other seventh and eighth graders: Sebastian, Leslie, Megan, and Michael. We order popcorn, Twizzlers, and sodas and head to the theater.

I bump into a familiar face walking out of theater number four—John.

I don't know why, but suddenly I feel my whole back fill with sweat. John is with his *abuela* and little brother. He says something to them and walks over to me. I tell Rachael and crew that I'll meet them inside.

"Hey, John. *¡Hola, Señora Lopez!*" I wave at his grandmother, and she waves back.

"Hey, yourself," John says.

We just kind of stand there staring at each other until John breaks the silence. "I see you're racking up in the friends department."

"Oh, Rachael? Yeah, she invited me. You know, just trying to show some of that Welcome-to-McManus spirit outside of school, I guess."

John doesn't look convinced. "Well, if you say so. Enjoy the movie. It was pretty epic."

Rachael peeks her head out the door to the theater and tells me to hurry it up.

John turns and starts walking toward his family.

"See you at school Monday!" I yell out.

But John doesn't even respond. He just throws up a peace sign and keeps walking.

I make my way inside, and just then I get a text message.

> **Mae:** Hey, stranger. Long time no text. Or Snapchat. Or FaceTime.

The houselights go out. There's no time to text back. Rachael loudly whispers, "Over here, Annabelle! I saved you a seat."

She saved me a seat all right. Right next to Bryan. And his bright smile and his perfect haircut and his perfect smell.

*Woodsy,* just like I thought.

I plop into the chair just before the movie begins.

Rachael nudges me in the side. "Aren't you glad I saved you from nerd boy?"

I look at her, confused. "What?"

"Don't act like you don't know what I'm talking about, girl. John is about as dorky as they come. Stick with me, kid. I'll move you up the ranks in no time."

Ranks? I'm not sure how high I want to climb.

# 4

# RETHINKING

Whoever invented bodysuits needs to be put on punishment. By fifth period, I'm so uncomfortable wearing this thing. Also, my feet hurt from the high-heeled booties Rachael picked out for me last Saturday. My mouth is dry from the matte lipstick she made me wear as we *put our faces on* in the bathroom before homeroom. And I'm pretty sure my hair has had enough of being fried every day just to stay straight.

Clairna and John stop me in the hallway just as the lunch bell rings.

"Are you going to come see us practice our band performance for the winter ball?" Clairna asks.

I see Rachael, Natasha, and Lauren coming my way.

"Sure thing, as soon as I'm done eating."

John and Clairna make their way to the gym, lunch bags in hand. I go to the cafeteria and shyly walk to the table Rachael has claimed as her rightful throne. Bryan is there. He smiles at me, but doesn't say a word. I smile back.

Rachael told me that Bryan wants to ask me to the dance. But other than a smile here or there, it's like he doesn't even know I exist. It doesn't matter anyway, because Dad would flip.

"What are you guys wearing to the winter ball?" Natasha kicks off the conversation.

"My favorite color, blue, of course," Lauren says.

Rachael says, "My mom is getting me a ball gown from Luxe in Woodbridge Mall."

I finally speak. "Sounds expensive."

"Four hundred dollars, if you call that expensive. How many times in our lives will we ever have a winter ball? Plus, you wouldn't catch me dead in the same dress more than once."

I think on that for a second. Does that mean I have to go shopping for more clothes? What I purchased with the girls won't last me through the winter at this rate! Maybe I can sneak back to the Second Chance store and find a dress for the winter ball.

Twenty minutes go by of everyone sitting there talking about the dance, how "lit" they're gonna look and how "lit" the school dance is going to be. The whole thing is giving my stomach a case of the heebie-jeebies. Aside from having to dress up, am I going to have to actually dance at this thing?

I decide right then and there that I'm not

going. And there's nothing Mom or Dr. Varma can say to convince me otherwise.

Just then, John and Clairna enter the cafeteria, and I can tell they're looking for me. Yikes! I forgot to go to the gym to see them practice.

John boldly walks to Rachael's table. Clairna lags behind.

Rachael stands up first. "Can I help you?"

"I need to talk to Annabelle," John says.

Rachael turns to me as if to ask if that's OK.

"Since when do I need permission to talk to my friend?" John asks.

Rachael sucks her teeth, but I jolt up and say, "It's fine. I'm sorry, John, I forgot."

"Yeah, I bet. You've been forgetting about a lot of things lately. Like who your real friends are."

"I'm her friend too, nerd boy," Rachael says.

Everybody at the table starts laughing.

I want to tell Rachael to stop, but my mouth

doesn't let me. Every single part of my face is frozen stiff.

John stands there, waiting to see if I'll do anything. And when I don't, he shakes his head at me, like I'm the biggest disappointment in the world. He walks back to Clairna, and together they leave the cafeteria. I mouth "I'm sorry" at her, but she doesn't even acknowledge me.

Maybe John's right. Maybe I need to rethink this whole friend thing.

# 5

# BLENDING

Things get weirder as the days go on. John, Clairna, and Nav barely speak to me anymore. My new wardrobe isn't comfortable at all. Like seriously, "cold shoulder" shirts are well . . . cool. Not in a good way! And to make things worse, I'm starting to notice that a lot of the girls at school dress the same. You can barely tell us apart.

Is this really what I want? To be a little soldier in the fashion diva army? To hang out with girls who like to tease my friends?

And for the first time, my inner Daphne and Annabelle become one: *This might not be what you signed up for, girl!*

During science lab, Mr. Friedank pairs us up. In today's experiment we're using rubber bands to test the effects of potential and kinetic energy to make a toy vehicle move.

"Annabelle, your partner will be John," Mr. Friedank says.

John lets out a long sigh and takes his place at the lab table next to me in the front of the class. Mr. Friedank gives further instructions and tells us to begin.

I start gathering the materials we need: K'Nex pieces and varying sizes of rubber bands, but the whole time I don't say anything to John.

There's some giggling coming from the left of our lab table. When I look over, I see it's Rachael and Natasha, and they're staring right at me. I raise my shoulders at them as if to say, "What's going on?" But then they start giggling some more. Rachael rips out a sheet of paper from her notebook and starts writing like a madwoman.

"You ready to work, or are you too busy with your new *squad*?" John asks, taking my attention away from Rachael and Natasha.

"I don't know what you're talking about," I say, snapping a connector to the front axle of the vehicle.

"Well, you know what they say?"

"What's that?" I ask.

Mrs. Gironda peeks her head into the classroom and asks Mr. Friedank to step into the hallway for a second. Rachael takes full advantage and flies a paper plane over to my table. I catch it in midair, fast before Mr. Friedank walks back in.

"The price of fame is expensive and will leave you broke," John responds.

"Who said that nonsense?" I twist my face and finally look at John. And when I do, the sun catches him right in the eyes, showing off a kaleidoscope of browns, grays, and greens.

"I don't know. I read it in a magazine." He shrugs.

I open the paper airplane, turning my back a little to John so he won't see. And when I read the message, my insides shrivel: *Step away from the dork, Annabelle. We wouldn't want to see you return to dork status.*

"What's with you these days?" John's question breaks me out of my thoughts.

I wonder the same. New clothes. New hair. New "squad." I'm not sure if I'm liking this new me after all.

I take the note, stuff it into my pocket, and glance at Rachael and Natasha, who are laughing uncontrollably now.

"Yeah, we never see you anymore," Clairna chimes in. She and Nav are partnered at the lab table behind us.

"It's like we need an appointment," Nav says.

I turn around, and he bows to me like I'm English royalty.

John throws in one more jab. "Guess we're not good enough for you anymore."

But that's not true! And Clairna pushed me to hang out with Rachael anyway! Why? So I could get an "in" with Steven Chu? (Who, by the way, suffers from the incurable disease of Immaturitis. After two days of sitting with him at lunch, the diagnosis was easy.)

I want to say all of that, but Rachael and Natasha's giggling is throwing my concentration off. And speaking of concentration, it doesn't even look like they've started their project.

"Oh, don't be like that, guys," I whisper. "Besides, Clairna, you made me go shopping with Rachael in the first place!"

"Shopping for clothes is one thing. Shopping for a whole new set of friends is different!"

Clairna gives me a major Rachael-level glare.

Ouch.

Mr. Friedank steps back inside the room and paces to our area to make sure we're doing the experiment. John completes the last steps—wrapping a thin rubber band around the toy vehicle's back axle eight times to see if it's enough to transform potential energy into kinetic. Four and six winds produced very little movement, if any. But eight times sends the vehicle flying off the lab table.

We record our notes on the lab sheet.

"Excellent work, John and Annabelle," Mr. Friedank says.

As soon as Mr. Friedank walks to the back of the lab, John starts up again. "When I first met you, I was like, 'Wow, a girl from Germany who's different and cool and not trying to fit in with anyone.' It's like you didn't have to be phony to make anyone like you."

Then Clairna adds her bit. "You don't need to wear certain things or hang out with a certain crowd to fit in. We liked you better when you were just yourself."

That last part really hurts, but I don't say anything back, because honestly, what can I say?

Class ends, and John, Clairna, and Nav grab their things and head to next period, leaving me behind.

# 6

# I ALREADY KNOW

My alarm goes off late the next morning. All of my new clothes are in the dirty clothes basket, which means I have to fish out something from my old wardrobe. Or raid Mom's closet, but she's not home to help me with this fashion emergency.

To make matters worse, the weather gods decided to be comedians today by painting the Linden skies gray with a dash of thunder clouds.

Dad yells from the front door, "Hurry up or I'm going to miss the train. I'll wait for you in the car!"

Quickly, I toss on a pair of brown overalls and a multi-colored plaid shirt. But I need *something* to cuten up the look, so I roll up the pants to my shins and throw on those high-heeled booties. The toaster oven starts screaming just as I draw in one squiggly eyebrow. Next thing I know, I'm flying down the steps to the kitchen, stuffing a burned bagel into my mouth, and darting to the car while the weather gods laugh and dump rain on every. Single. Part of me.

By the time I get to school, I look a HOT, RAINY, MUDDY POODLE-HAIR MESS!

Rachael and friends waste no time letting me know. "What on earth happened to you, girl?" she greets me in the hallway, her crew around her smirking.

I feel the tips of my ears ignite and stay burning for the rest of the day.

At lunch I walk over to their table and even though there's a spot to sit, Rachael tells me: "Sorry, there's no room."

My inner Daphne voice chimes in: *So let me get this straight. I ditch my friends to hang out with you. I change my fashions and am finally "accepted" by you. And the one day I can't dress to your approval, I'm not good enough to sit with you?*

That's it. I'm done with Rachael.

Of course I don't say any of that. My inner Annabelle won't let me. Being shy can be such a thrill-kill sometimes!

So I walk away in a huff. I don't care about trying to walk like some supermodel, and I don't care about wearing clothes that make me look diva-esque and give me wedgies.

Just then I see John, Clairna, and Nav look at me and then go back to pretending that they're enjoying today's lunch: Veggie Surprise.

LIARS!!!

Clearly, even they don't want me at their lunch table. I'm not sure I can blame them after the way I've been treating them. So I storm out of the cafeteria and go to the next best hiding spot: the paper supply closet.

And Nav is right . . . the smell of new paper is AMAZING!

I pull out my phone and text Mae. Lately, I've been slow to respond to her texts, or I've just not been responding at all. I can handle losing Rachael as a friend, even John, but not Mae.

**Me:** Hey. Sorry I've been such a bad friend lately.

Two minutes pass. Then five. My heart sinks with the tick of each second that passes. But then . . .

**Mae:** It's OK, *amiga*! I've been busy too. Working on something big. More on that later.

But tell me . . . how is my superstar friend?

I breathe the biggest sigh of relief. At least one friend isn't mad at me. I tell Mae all about this latest Daphne experiment, how annoying the whole fashion thing is, how mean Rachael is, and how I think I've lost the only friends I've made at McManus.

**Mae:** I think you know what you have to do.

Mae's right. I know exactly how I'm going to fix all of this. I squeeze my eyes closed really tight and pray for dismissal to hurry up so this day can be over with already. There's a new vlog waiting to be recorded.

But first, I need to try to make things right.

**Belle** to Group, John, Clairna, Nav:

Hey, guys. I'm sorry. For everything. I'm going back to just being myself.

Can we start over and be friends again?

Ten minutes later . . .

*seen by all*

No response.

# 7

# DAPHNE DOESN'T DO FASHION

As soon as I get home, I transform myself into Daphne—lime green wig with glitter strands, my Harry Potter–style cape, an oversized hat with a feather, and pink-rimmed shades that are about five times too big for my face. I look ridiculous, but I am loving every part of my outfit.

Today I decide I'm going live.

Now that my channel has grown to over ten thousand subscribers, YouTube allows this feature. I'm way too anxious about everything that happened at school today to spend time editing in iMovie. I need to get some stuff off my chest before I spontaneously combust.

I set my phone on the tripod, open the app, start playing music and dancing, and I don't even care that I have zero rhythm. Going live in three . . . two . . . one . . .

"Hi, guys! It's your girl, Daphne, and welcome to my channel, *Daphne Doesn't*.

"Today's episode is all about fashion and the top five things I can't stand about following the latest trends:

"Number one: The expense. People of YouTube land, shop the clearance rack! Who spends hundreds of dollars on shoes? Or even worse, seventy-five hundred dollars on a coat? Do you realize how many tech gadgets I could get with that kind of money? Thrift shops exist, people. You can probably find that same coat in a thrift shop for *wayyy* cheaper.

"Number two: Rips, rips everywhere!

People! Why are we buying purposely ripped clothes? It's cold outside. It's almost Christmas, for crying out loud! So cover up and let it snow, let it snow, let it snow! Geez!

"Number three: Bodysuits. The nineties called, and they want their onesies back! These things need to be a criminal offense. Just trust me when I tell you to *never ever* wear them. Your butt will thank you.

"Number four: Wavy eyebrows. Now I don't mean eyebrows that naturally grow wavy and there's nothing you can do about it. I'm talking about dipping a toothbrush in hair gel to purposely transform your eyebrows into waves that even mermaids would want to swim in. Just . . . don't.

"Number five: And my least favorite one of all? Blending in. There is no individuality when you're trying to look like everyone else. Where's the fun in that?

"It's cool to be different. It's OK to be

yourself. Even if that means some people will make you feel bad about it. So wave your inner fashion weirdo flag high and mighty, because trends may come and go, but individuality lasts forever.

"Thanks for watching *Daphne Doesn't*. Be sure to like, follow, and subscribe. See you on the next episode!"

During the whole taping, I see the views increase. Fourteen hundred and forty-one, then eight thousand, then twenty-seven thousand and counting.

The comments start flooding in:

**LifeWithDogs:** I think following fashion trends is silly too! Just be yourself!

**PinkyHearts:** Who cares what's on the outside? It's what's inside that matters.

**Elle_Sauly:** Cool dance moves, Daphne!

**BrooklynChica:** OMG, please do a vlog just about that silly squiggle-brow!

That last comment sparks an itch to give the people what they want. So I do another live vlog showing everyone just how horrific squiggly eyebrows can look. And between the two new vlogs, the comments keep rolling in. Funny requests. Positive vibes. All of it makes me feel like what I'm doing means something.

But even though shooting the live vlogs felt like the most amazing release, another familiar feeling soon returns—emptiness. John, Clairna, and Nav haven't responded to my text message, but they all saw it. And now I have a feeling that I blew my shot at real friendship. Because I didn't speak up, I messed it all up. I'm not cut out for school or sports or drama or fashion. But worst of all? I'm not cut out for friends.

It's almost ten o'clock by the time I finish

hanging out in my girl cave listening to depressing Ed Sheeran songs.

"Time to close up shop, Annabelle!" Dad yells down the basement steps, just as I'm shutting down my MacBook.

"Coming, Dad."

When I get upstairs, Dad is sitting at the breakfast bar, drinking hot tea. "What's with the glum face?" he asks.

I turn off the basement lights and close the door. Then I pull up a stool and join him at the counter. "It's just things are . . . complicated," I admit.

Dad takes a sip of his tea, and the warm, gingery smell spreads all around the space between us. "I thought things were going well. Aren't you happy? You're Miss Popularity now."

"I'm not sure if any of it matters. The clothes. The fake friends. I felt more like myself when I hung out with John, Clairna, and Nav. Now I think they hate me. And honestly, I'm not sure if *I* like me like this either." By the last word, I'm crying.

Dad puts his tea down and pulls me in for a hug, where I let it all out. Tears, fears, and a few sobs. "It doesn't matter how other people see you," he says. "All that matters is how you see yourself. As for your old friends, I'm sure things will get better really soon. Say, since Mom's at Fort Dix doing overtime, it's a Daddy-daughter weekend. You know you could invite your friends over, if you want. My kitchen is always open."

My father, Señor Ruben Louis, aka the BEST dad in the world, just gave me an idea. I know exactly how I'll fix things!

# 8

# BEING NORMAL

I go back to school Friday dressed as my normal self. Rachael can have the popularity, the fashion, and the teasing.

As I walk into homeroom, I can feel all eyes on me. And it takes me right back to the first day of school.

Counting the tiles on the floor, walking to my seat in the back of the room, hearing the whispers:

"What happened to Annabelle?"

"Looks like she's back to her old self."

"Pick a team, girl. Dope or Dork."

I sink into my chair, trying to block out the comments and the googly eyes. When I do take my eyes off the floor, I notice John staring at me. And not in the *I-still-hate-you* way, but more like a *nice-to-see-the-real-you-again* kinda way.

It starts with a smile, even though it's faint. By second period, it's a casual "hey" from John, Clairna, and then Nav. By third period, it's a "See you at lunch?" from John, which I take as a sign that maybe he's not mad at me anymore.

This makes me feel a thousand times better! No more eating in the paper supply closet.

Before lunch, I stop at my locker to switch books. Clairna is at her locker too.

"You sitting with us today, or what?" she says, grabbing her algebra book.

My smile grows and circles around the

circumference of my head. "After you guys didn't respond to my text, I thought . . . Listen, I'm sorry if I—"

Clairna holds her hand in the air and cuts me off. "Apologies aren't necessary. I get it. You took a drink from the popular jug. It tasted good at first, until that aftertaste settled on your tongue. And I admit, I'm the one who pushed you in that direction, for my own selfish reasons. Turns out Steve Chu has the maturity level of a seven-year-old!"

I start laughing. "I totally agree!"

We slap high fives, and everything feels right in my world again.

"I'll meet you guys in the cafeteria. I have to use the bathroom first."

"Sure thing." Clairna starts making her way to the cafeteria.

When I enter the bathroom, who do I see staring in the mirror, *putting her face on*?

Rachael stops midgloss and tosses the tube into her pink, fuzzy makeup bag. I pay her no mind and handle my business. I take my time, hoping she'll walk out of the bathroom any second now, or that one of her fans will come in and distract her. But under the stall I can see her feet glued in place, like she's waiting for me.

When I'm done, I go to the sink to wash my hands, not looking her way. I wash my hands extra fast, because I just want to get out of there. But then Rachael can't take my ignoring her. She corners me, putting her face so close to mine, I can smell her lip gloss—a mixture of candy canes and something fruity. Must be new.

"Nice outfit, Annabelle."

My soul dies a little, but I refuse to let her see it. "Um, thanks." I inch a little to the left. Rachael follows.

"Check out this YouTube live video." She shoves her iPhone in my face.

I pretend like I'm watching it for the first time.

"Funny, huh?" she asks.

And then she swipes her phone and shows the eyebrow vlog. That's when I know I'm toast.

"Yeah, that girl is pretty hilarious," I say, trying to play it off.

"Hmm . . . so funny because Daphne is showing the eyebrow trick exactly like the way I showed you," Rachael says.

I don't respond, just kinda nod like, *yeah, that's so crazy, girl!*

But Rachael's not done with me yet. "Say, doesn't that necklace look familiar?" She pauses the video and zooms in.

My hands rise up to my neck. Mom's necklace. The same necklace I forgot to take off last night for my vlog! But there's no way I'm telling Rachael that, so I just lie: "Sort of, I guess. But you can find this necklace at any store. And there's lots of makeup vlogs on YouTube. Daphne could've learned that trick anywhere."

"Oh yeah? Same words and everything, huh? Nice cover-up, Annabelle."

"What do you mean?"

*And cue sweaty back!*

"It all makes sense now. You, re-enacting the same scene from *Little Shop of Horrors* and then stealing my part from me. Your mom calling you 'Daph.' That YouTube comment about Daphne living right here in New Jersey. And now you're wearing the exact same necklace. I'm not stupid. I know you're Daphne!"

I laugh out loud, trying my best to convince Rachael—and myself—that she's got it wrong. "You've officially lost it, girl."

The second I say that I can't believe it. I've never been so snippy with anyone.

"Nice comeback, dorkface. Way to dodge the accusation."

My stomach hurts because I know I'm about to tell a huge lie.

"It's not me." I can't breathe. My nerves are

piling up in my stomach, and any second I'm going to let them all out.

"Well, we'll just see about that, won't we?" Then Rachael storms out of the bathroom.

# 9

# NO MORE HIDING

I can't even think about showing my face in the cafeteria. By now, I'm sure Rachael has told every single one of her friends. And I can't bear the thought of them staring and pointing and whispering. So I do what I've now become an expert at: I hide.

One place I know Rachael wouldn't be caught dead in is the library. Mrs. Ransome, our school librarian, makes this a place where we can really escape. Signs are posted all around: *McManus scholars are building our future!* There are plenty of tables with chairs in the middle of the library and comfortable sofas lining the wall of windows. And to top it off, light classical music plays softly in the background.

Thankfully, the library is almost empty—just two students seated at separate tables and Mrs. Ransome, who greets me with a welcoming smile. I take a seat on the oversized comfy couch in front of the window with the big pine tree. I pull out my MacBook from my knapsack, open up an old video folder, and randomly select one.

I don't notice when John walks into the library, but I feel his touch when he taps me on the shoulder. "Nice video. Where's it from?" he asks.

It's a clip of Mae and me doing voiceovers, re-enacting a scene from *Star Wars* using action figures. An oldie but goodie.

"I made it," I say.

John slides into the seat next to me to take a closer look. I breathe in and catch a whiff of his scent.

*Woodsy.*

"That's amazing. Your impersonations are spot on. How d'you do that?"

"I can speak in many accents," I say, and then I stop talking because thoughts of Daphne and my perfectly cheeky British accent come up.

"You should make a YouTube channel!" he says.

I take in a large breath.

I should tell him the truth before Rachael does. Right now. Stop hiding. Get it over with.

Instead I say, "I'm sorry for not being a better friend."

I want to tell him what happened in the bathroom with Rachael, but for some reason I don't.

John scans my face, as though he's waiting

for me to say more. "I know you are. You don't need to hole yourself up in the library or the paper closet every day."

"How'd you know?" I ask.

"Navdeep caught you going in there last week, when *he* was looking for a place to hide."

We burst out laughing. And finally it feels like I have some sense of normalcy again. But there's that tug in my stomach returning. I've got to say something before Rachael opens her big mouth and starts spreading my secret.

And just when I'm ready to say something, in walk Clairna and Nav.

"Annabelle, what's up? We were waiting for you in the cafeteria," Nav says, taking a seat on the carpet.

"Yeah, what happened?" Clairna asks, sitting beside him. "I told you we were cool again. What'd you do? Get nervous?"

I shrug.

Here's my chance to get it all out in front of my friends. But what if they react like Rachael did? Or worse? Then I really will spend the rest of the school year hiding in the paper supply closet.

"Friends again?" John holds out his fist for a bump.

"You got it." I bump fists with him.

It's then that I hear Mae's and Dad's voices echo in my head. Their subtle reminders that things will get better and that they know I'll figure it all out. That's when I come up with a brilliant idea. "How about we have a pizza party tomorrow? My house?" I ask.

Nav's eyes brighten. "Pizza is my favorite food group."

Clairna and John chime in, adding in their favorite toppings. Pepperoni. Mushrooms. Nav adds pineapples. I'm not so sure about that last one.

Just then, Mr. Davis rushes into the library

with a box full of posters with snowflakes and other wintry pictures.

"Ah, thank goodness I found you, Annabelle, Clairna! Nicholas Rocco is out sick," Mr. Davis says, before he trips on a section of elevated carpet.

Some of the papers and markers spill out of the box and onto the floor. We all rush to help him pick them up. Mr. Davis breathes a sigh of relief and plops onto the couch next to us.

"Am I in trouble or something?" I ask.

"Quite the opposite!" he says. "I need your help. Actually, I can use all the help I can get right now. I tell you, a teacher's work is never done. Last month, it was directing the school play; this month, it's setting up for the Student-Parent Winter Ball. Add in the mounds of history papers I have to grade and the fact that I have two little people at home still in diapers, and I can't tell my right foot from my left foot these days. I digress."

Mr. Davis comes up for air and then continues. "You two did such an amazing job last month building the set for *Little Shop of Horrors,* not to mention the double duty of acting in it, Annabelle. I was hoping you could do me a huge favor and help with decorations for the winter ball next week. I'm heading the planning committee."

Clairna springs to her knees, excited about the request. "I'll help!"

Then everyone looks at me, waiting for an answer. I'm hesitant because I have no plans of going to the ball. But then I realize that I wouldn't have to actually *go,* I could just help set it up.

So I say, "Of course we'll help you, Mr. Davis." I turn to Clairna, Nav, and John. "I guess tomorrow will be a pizza and Winter Ball decorating party?"

Mr. Davis lets out a huge sigh of relief and then hands the box of decorations to me.

"See you guys at six o'clock," I say.

"You got it," John says. "See you then."

Tomorrow, I will hang out with my real friends. No squiggly eyebrows, name-brand jeans, or cherry bomb lip gloss needed.

# 10

# I GOT SOME 'SPLAININ' TO DO

Thank goodness for the weekend. It gives me time to take my mind off of Rachael's drama and set up for my pizza-slash-winter-ball-decorating party with John, Clairna, and Nav.

Dad goes easy on me this time. No complaints about boys. He helps me clean the house and decide what pizzas he'll make for my friends: pepperoni for John and me, mushroom for Clairna since she's a vegetarian, and Nav can eat that whole pineapple pizza by himself. Yuck!

The doorbell rings at six o'clock sharp.

"Cool house!" Clairna says as soon as everyone walks in.

"Thanks!" I blush.

That reminds me to make sure I shut the door to the basement. I make a mental note to do that in a few minutes.

For the next hour and a half, we settle down at our decorating station in the dining room.

We work on all of the decorations from Mr. Davis's box, starting with the snowflakes. There are hundreds of these. We cut them out and use glue to add silver glitter. Next up are the snowmen, which need different patterns and colors for the scarves.

When we're halfway done, Dad heads to the kitchen and fires up the oven to start making the pizzas.

"Dude, your dad is actually making the pizza?" Nav asks.

The delicious smells start to drift from the kitchen to the dining room.

"Oh yeah, no ordering food in here. Dad cooks just about everything homemade," I say.

"You should have been here last time when me and Rachael came here to work on our group history project," John says. "Mr. Louis was making Spanish and German food."

My spirits drop when I hear him say Rachael's name, knowing that, come Monday, I will need a plan to deal with her once and for all.

Clairna hands me a pair of scissors to cut out the snowmen we've already decorated. "Speaking of Rachael, I have some scoop!"

Here it comes. I just know it.

"What's that?" John asks.

"The royal queen of McManus is upset that the king of eighth grade didn't ask her to the winter ball."

"Who? Ahmad Patel?" Nav says. "I'm cool with him. We're in the same karate class, and trust me, he has no interest in her."

"Pizzas are almost done!" Dad yells from the kitchen.

"Smells delicious, Mr. Louis!" John calls out.

"So . . . who are you going to the winter ball with?" Clairna looks straight at me.

And suddenly, it's like the whole world pauses.

The holiday music stops playing from the speakers.

Nav and John stop cutting snowmen.

Dad stops cooking in the kitchen. I can *feel* him listening.

"Um, I'm not going."

John's jaw nearly falls onto the dining table. "What do you mean, not going?"

"Oh come on, Annabelle. You have to go!" Nav says, "Clairna and I are going together . . . as friends."

Clairna smiles shyly.

Dad walks in, as if on cue, wiping his saucy hands on his apron.

"You and John should go to the winter ball *together*!" Clairna says it like it's the brightest idea she's ever had.

I keep cutting, pretending that I didn't hear her, and also that Dad is invisible. I'm expecting him to embarrass me any second. In three . . . two . . .

"That's a good idea, Clairna, especially since parents are invited as well," Dad says with a wink.

*Please don't make this moment any weirder than it already is!*

I stop cutting and look at the floor. And then at John. And there's that smile and that dimple again, sinking all the way to his shiny, brace-covered teeth.

I let out a small cough.

Then another one follows and another and another. Clairna hands me a bottle of water. I take a large gulp and let it all sink in.

"If you don't want to go to the dance with me, that's cool. I'm bringing my *abuela* anyway." John shrugs.

"No, no! I want to go," I finally speak. "It's just that I . . . I don't know how to dance."

"That's OK! Neither do I," John says. "I might be the only Puerto Rican on earth with no rhythm."

Dad starts giggling and points at me. "Make that two."

"Dad!" My cheeks flame up, but I'm laughing too.

"I can show you guys how to dance salsa!" Dad presses a button on the remote, and the stereo switches to a song by Marc Anthony.

He starts moving and twirling to "Vivir Mi Vida" as though he's dancing with Mom, even though she's not here.

And then John, Clairna, and Nav join in the dancing.

For the whole song, there they are—my friends and my dad—dancing and laughing as Marc Anthony sings about living your life, through good and bad times.

When the song ends, Dad lowers the volume. "Looks like you guys are just about done with the decorations. Ready to eat?"

We all scream, "Yeah!" and clear the table to make room for the pizzas.

Dad sends me to the garage to grab more water bottles while he lays out his masterpieces: three homemade pizzas, a tray of fettuccine alfredo, garden salad, and fudge brownies.

When I come in from the garage, I notice

it's just Dad and Nav standing in the dining room.

"Where'd everyone go?" I ask.

Nav points left. "Clairna is washing her hands in the bathroom."

"And I sent John to the . . ." Dad slows every single word, "half bathroom in the basement."

I dart out of the dining room, flames firing up in my ears.

Dad loudly whispers, "SORRY!"

My legs zip to the kitchen, hoping that I'll catch John just in time. But the door to the basement is wide open, the lights on the stairs are in full glow, and John is already in my girl cave.

I huff and puff as I get to my door and find him standing there, touching the rack of Daphne clothes, brushing his fingers across the couch, the sign, the art, every single part that screams I HAVE BEEN LYING!

His back is still turned to me, but I can tell he feels my presence.

"I think I owe you an explanation."

"Well, it's about time."

finitely doesn't do sports Def
n't do drama Definitely does
nitely doesn't do fashion De
ances Definitely doesn't do da
finitely doesn't do sports Spo
n't do drama Definitely does
nitely doesn't do fashion De
o dances Definitely doesn't d
y doesn't do sports Definitely
n't do drama Definitely does
nitely doesn't do fashion De
nces Definitely doesn't do Fas
y doesn't do sports Definitel
n't do drama Definitely does
finitely doesn't do Sports De
nces Definitely doesn't do Fas

# TALK ABOUT IT!

1. Annabelle wants to be friends with Rachael and her fashionable group, but doing so pushes her away from her real friends. Why do you think it was so tough for Annabelle to go back to her true self?

2. When Annabelle tries to make things right and apologize to John, Clairna, and Nav, they don't respond to her at first. Have you ever had to apologize and received a similar reaction? Did you feel the same way as Annabelle did?

3. Rachael shows a more real side of herself when she talks to Annabelle about her dad's deployment. Why do you think she still fights with Annabelle even when they have this in common?

# WRITE IT DOWN!

1. As soon as Annabelle doesn't dress as fashionably as Rachael and her group, they treat her like she was never their friend. Write a letter from Annabelle's perspective responding to them.

2. Rachael pieces together the clues and finds out that Annabelle is also Daphne. Annabelle says she isn't, but Rachael isn't convinced. Write about what you think would happen if Annabelle told Rachael the truth.

3. Annabelle has a new costume for each Daphne video. Write down what you would want for your costume if you were making Daphne-style vlogs.